ALIEN TEETH

by

Ian MacDonald

Essex County Council Libraries

First Published
September 07 in Great Britain by

PUBLISHING

ISBN-10: 1-905637-32-2
ISBN-13: 978-1-905637-32-4

Educational Printing Services Limited
Albion Mill, Water Street, Great Harwood, Blackburn BB6 7QR
Telephone: (01254) 882080   Fax: (01254) 882010
E-mail: enquiries@eprint.co.uk   Website: www.eprint.co.uk

Contents

Chapter 1
The Den

Sometimes, when you are stung by a bee, the sting stays in. That's what people say.

Owen didn't know it was the same with teeth.

But then he did not know anything about alien teeth.

* * *

Owen and Freddie looked up at the plastic sheet that was supposed to keep the rain out. There was a big hole and water was dripping in, making a puddle on the floor of the den. The den was the gang's hide-out. It was on a patch of waste ground and was built with some hardboard, a fence panel and a couple of old, wooden doors.

"Open up, will you?" came a voice from outside. It was Chaz.

"Open it yourself."

"Can't. I got my hands full."

Owen stood up and opened the door to the den. He did not exactly open it. To get into the den you had to lift the door out of the way, step inside and put the door back in the hole where the door went.

Chaz staggered through the doorway carrying a large bundle of newspapers tied with string.

"What on earth . . . ?" blinked Owen.

"I found it in the alley by the shops. Someone just dumped it there, didn't want it."

Chaz heaved the bundle onto the wooden box that was their table. Owen pulled one of the newspapers out of the bundle and read the date.

"It's today's newspaper, you cloth-brain!" said Owen. "The alley is where the van drops off the papers for the newspaper shop in the mornings. Look, it's *The Wormhill Echo!*"

"Don't worry," said Freddie, "they'll just think someone's stolen it, that's all."

"Someone has stolen it, you wombat!" said Owen. "Chaz has stolen it! The police are probably out looking for him now."

But neither Chaz nor Freddie was taking Owen seriously.

"Here look at this . . . **UFO SCARES FARMER'S SHEEP**," read Freddie, pulling a paper from the bundle. "What about this . . . ? **FILM STAR TO JUDGE PET CONTEST.** Famous film star Dirk Vapour will be guest of honour at the village show. He will give out prizes, including a tour of the film-set for his next film, Alien Invasion."

"Look, if we get the papers back to the shop they might not say anything," said Owen, snatching the papers from Freddie.

"Never mind that," said Chaz, "how did Rovers get on on Saturday?" He snatched the paper from Owen and turned to the back page. "FOUR-NIL!" shouted Chaz. "Champions! Champions!"

With that Chaz tore out a handful of newspaper and scrunched it into a large ball. He dropped it to the floor and took a swing with his foot. The paper ball took off and bounced off Owens's head.

"Stop!" said Owen. "You're making it worse."

But Chaz took no notice. Instead, he moved two boxes a couple of paces apart and waved Freddie in goal. "And the ball is floated across to Jasper Stokes, the Rover's striker. He shoots . . . it's there! He's scored! Four-nil to Rovers!"

"That's enough," shouted Owen.

Chaz and Freddie stopped. The paper football rolled across the floor and stopped in a puddle. Owen picked it up and tried to wipe off some of the mud.

"Come on," Owen said, picking up the rest of the bundle, "we're taking this lot back to the newspaper shop. Are you two coming?"

Freddie put his hands in his pockets.

"It's your fault, both of you!" added Owen crossly.

Chaz scuffed at the ground with his trainers, not looking up.

"Fine, I'll do it myself!" snapped Owen. He picked up the bundle of newspapers and stomped out of the den.

Chapter Two
U.F.O.

Owen made his way along the rough track that crossed the waste ground behind the housing estate. The quickest way to the shops was through the estate, past a lot of houses. Someone might see him. They might wonder what a boy was doing with a large bundle of newspapers.

Owen rested the bundle of newspapers on the ground for a moment. They did not look so good now. Some of the pages were torn and falling out. There were splashes of mud everywhere. But it would have to do.

Owen decided to cut behind the railway line to get to the shops. There was less chance of being spotted that way. It would take longer, that was all. And it meant cutting across Stockett's Farm. That was O.K. unless you bumped into the farmer. Some people said he chased some boys with a stick once. But it was worth the risk.

There were worse things you could meet than farmers.

* * *

It was then that he saw it. Hovering above the dark trees was a spaceship! It was shaped like two saucers stuck together.

All along the outer edge were small
bumps, making it look as if the two halves
had been bolted together in a car factory.

There did not appear to be any windows on the spaceship, and no light showed anywhere on its surface. But underneath it the ground was lit up with a bright white light, like a football pitch with floodlights. The whole thing was dark grey, the colour of metal that has been left in the rain. It had the appearance of something bought from a second-hand spaceship salesman.

Owen dropped the newspapers and started to run towards the spaceship. His feet splashed in muddy puddles spattering his jeans with brown splodges. A few cows, munching on grass, looked up for a moment before returning to their lunch. Reaching the other side of the field, he scrambled through a gap in the hedge. The prickly twigs tore a hole in his jacket sleeve.

Owen plunged on into the wood. He dodged in and out of the trees, scrambled over fallen branches and squelched through a carpet of fallen leaves. It was much darker here than out in the fields. A few crows, startled by the boy running below them, flapped into the air, their calls echoing against the trees.

And then the ground began to shake.

The spaceship.

It must be going.

Nearly there now.

Keep going.

Owen ran hard and leapt at the fence that marked the end of the wood. He thought he had cleared it but his foot just caught the top as he came over, and he fell heavily on the wet ground. Owen looked up.

There was someone moving on the other side of the bushes. The figure was a dark shape against the bright light from the spaceship.

"Who's there?" called Owen.

The figure seemed startled by the voice. It stopped still for a moment and peered back at Owen through the branches. Then it turned and scuttled away towards the light.

Owen scrambled to his feet.

Everything about him was moving: the trees bent almost to the ground and even the ground seemed to tremble.

Chapter Three

A Pain in the Backside

Then the air seemed to ripple and shake. It was as if everything about him were being sucked towards the light. Owen grabbed hold of a nearby bush and clung on. He looked up, straining his eyes against the bright light. Suddenly, with a blast of hot air, the spaceship zoomed upwards - and was gone.

Owen fell backwards.

"Ouch!"

He had just sat down on something sharp. He scrambled up and looked back at the tree stump behind him. There was nothing there. But he was still in pain - something was biting his bottom!

Owen spun around, like a dog chasing his tail. He fully expected to see a squirrel, or some other woodland creature, hanging off the back of his trousers. But there was nothing to see. He wafted his hands behind him. Still nothing! He clamped his hands right where the pain was.

Owen gasped.

There was something there. Something about the size of a large apple and smooth

like a stone. And it was attached to Owen.
Whatever it was had sunk itself into his
flesh right through his jeans. Owen tugged
at the object.

"Ouch!"

He tried again.

"Oooowww!"

Owen bent forward, reached between his legs and grabbed hold of the object with both hands. He gave a last mighty heave.

"Aaaaaarggghh!!"

The thing came away in his hands.

Owen looked.

It was a set of teeth!

* * *

Back home Owen went to his room and, with the help of two mirrors, inspected the damage to his rear end. Once he had patched himself up he reached into his pocket and took out the offending object.

It certainly was a set of teeth, there was no mistake about that, but unlike anything Owen had seen before.

Owen went to the mirror and curled his lips back. He held the strange teeth up beside his own. The whole set were bigger than his. The front teeth, however, did not look very different. The rest of the teeth all around the edge were much like his own, but smoother, almost as if they had been polished.

There was one difference. Owen saw that he had a pointy tooth either side of his four front teeth. This set, however, had a pair of teeth like this on both sides; and these teeth were much larger and curved in towards the middle. There was something else, too. These teeth were perfect. They looked like they had never been used.

"Wow, what a pair of gnashers!" gasped Freddie.

"Not so loud!" hissed Owen. "You'll have Old Potts over!"

"How did you make them?" said Chaz.

"I didn't make them. I found them."

"Found them?"

"Well, sort of . . . they kind of found me, really."

Chaz and Freddie looked blank.

"They, er . . . bit me on the bottom."

The two friends cupped their hands over their mouths to muffle their laughter.

"You mean an animal bit you and left its teeth in your . . ."

"There wasn't an animal."

"You mean these teeth just crept up on you, and bit you on the bottom?"

More laughter.

"What's that you've got there, boys?"

It was Mr Potts.

Chapter Four
"Where's my Teeth?"

"Oh, nothing, Sir."

"It's teeth, Mr Potts."

"I can see that, Frederick."

"Do you think they're dinosaur teeth, Sir?"

Chaz made a monster face at Owen behind the teacher's back.

"I doubt it. I've got a book about fossils somewhere. Maybe I can check for you later. Now, perhaps you can finish your writing about the force of gravity, if you're not too busy?"

* * *

In the afternoon they were in the computer room. Freddie and Chaz were sharing a computer and Owen was working next to them.

"So where did you get those teeth, then?"

"I told you. I found them in the wood, over Stockett's Farm."

"What, were they just hanging in a tree, or something?"

"Well," said Owen, turning a bit red,

"you know that newspaper story about a spaceship . . . "

"Argghh, Owen's had his brain stolen by aliens. He's gone completely bonkers!" laughed Freddie.

"Far too much noise, boys," said Mrs Hart, coming over to see what all the fuss was about. "Look, there's nothing in your note-books, boys. Owen, you try that spare computer over there."

"But, Miss!"

The teacher looked stern. The three boys split up.

Owen went to the corner by himself. He pressed the button on the screen monitor. Nothing happened. Then the screen crackled and snowed black and white, like a TV not tuned to a channel.

"Miss, it's not . . . "

And then the screen cleared. It went green . . . and purple lettering wrote itself across the screen.

WHERE'S . . . MY . . . TEETH!

Owen looked around.

"Chaz," he hissed, "stop mucking about."

But Chaz was busy on his computer. So was Freddie. Owen looked around the room. No one was sniggering behind hands. He looked back at the screen just as the message faded and the screen went black.

"Try plugging it in, sunshine," said Ken the technician, leaning over Owen's desk. He bent under the desk and put a plug in a socket. The screen hummed into life.

* * *

Back home Grandad was watching the football.

"Hello Owen. Arsenal's one up."

"Be down later, Grandad," called Owen, "just got some homework to do upstairs."

Owen shut the door of his room.

He took the teeth out of his pocket and turned them in his hands.

After school Mr Potts had told him that he had not been able to find a match for the teeth in his book. He had even tried searching a natural history data-base on the Internet, but nothing looked anything like the strange teeth. Owen was sure that the teeth had something to do with the spaceship.

He had the alien's teeth!

And someone wanted them back.

"Owen. Dinner's ready. Wash your hands, please," Mum called from downstairs.

Owen put the teeth back in his pocket and wandered into the bathroom. He turned the tap on and gave his hands a quick splash.

On the window sill in front of him was a glass. In the glass were Grandad's false teeth. Owen reached in and lifted them out. He took the teeth from his pocket and held both sets up together. He ran his fingers over the surface. Grandad's teeth felt rough and a bit slimy. The others felt perfectly smooth and clean.

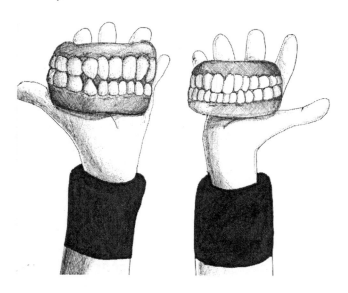

There was a knock at the door.

"Owen!"

"Coming!"

Owen dropped Grandad's teeth back in the glass and quickly ran downstairs.

At dinner he made up his mind.

He must return the teeth.

Chapter Five
Emperor Zarg

Owen stood in the darkness, waiting.
His hand went again to his jeans pocket,
checking the scrunched-up plastic bag was
still there. The wind moaned sadly through
the woods behind him; a few crows cawed at
the tops of tall trees; otherwise, the fields
for miles around were silent.

Owen sat down on a tree stump,
checking it first for strange objects.

"This is stupid," thought Owen, "even if there is an alien out there, how is he going to know I'm here?"

Owen stood up to leave. And then the air began to vibrate. The trees began to sway. The ground started to shake. Owen had to shield his eyes as the whole area was flooded with white light.

"Welcome here, Earthling," said a voice, "may I invite you on board my excellent craft?"

"No thanks, if it's all the same to you," stammered Owen. His hand went to his pocket. Owen had decided to leave the teeth on the tree stump where he had found them. But it all happened too quickly.

"Bow down before his Excellency, The Emperor Zarg, High Commander of the Zargon Fleet."

Owen blinked and rubbed his eyes. He was standing in an enormous room. The metal floors, walls and ceiling shone like mirrors, making it hard to see. Owen had the feeling there were other people in the room, but it was hard to tell how many. As his eyes began to focus he saw that he was standing by a tall cylinder, which towered high above his head.

Seated on the cylinder was a creature. It was human in shape with two arms, two legs, hands and feet. Its face looked like melted wax. A large forehead bulged out over two narrow slits for eyes.

"I believe you have something that belongs to me, Earthchild," said the creature, yellow spit dribbling from its purple lips like pizza cheese.

"I didn't mean to take them. I just

sort of . . . sat on them," said Owen, hesitating. Perhaps it was not a good thing to tell an alien emperor that you had sat on his teeth. "I've got them here."

Owen reached into his pocket and pulled out the plastic bag. A few marbles spilled out of his pocket and rolled across the floor. The creature looked down and raised a fold of skin where an eyebrow should have been.

"Well?"

Owen could now see the other creatures standing behind Zarg, watching with interest. Some of them held what seemed to be rods of a bright material which crackled and sparkled like lightning in their clawed hands. Owen had the feeling they might be weapons.

"Here you are," he gulped, and peeled back the plastic to reveal a set of false teeth. They were slightly yellow and attached to pink gums. There was definitely a bit of beef-burger stuck between the two front teeth.

"Oh no," groaned Owen.

"What is this?" snarled Zarg.

"Um, there seems to have been a bit of a mix up, Your Majesty."

Zarg waved his hand. One of the creatures walked forward, picked the teeth up between two clawed fingers and held them up to the Emperor.

"What is the meaning of this? Have you brought me here to play games?"

"No . . . they're my grandad's teeth. There's been a slight mistake."

"Enough!"

Suddenly the floor seemed to open. Owen stepped back to stop himself from falling. He looked down. Where there should have been woods and trees and fields there was a lake of bubbling lava, flames shooting high into the air.

Owen wobbled as a jet of fire scorched his eyebrows.

"Wait!"

It was a girl's voice.

Owen turned to see a girl enter the room. She was just a little taller than Owen and he found her strangely beautiful.

Perhaps it was the way the eye in the middle of her forehead caught the light from the flames.

"Let him go," said the girl.

"Altar, my child, this is not for you to say," said Zarg.

"Let the Earthling go," said the girl. "I am sure he will return your precious teeth to you. If you do not, you may never see them again."

"Yes, good idea. I'll go now shall I?" said Owen.

"Silence, Earthchild," Zarg lifted a hand to his face, and stroked the hole that was his nose. "Perhaps you are right, my daughter. Very well - seven days, and I will return. Do not disappoint me. Or this is what I will do to your tiny planet."

Zarg made a fist around Grandad's teeth and squeezed. There was the sound of crunching. A white powder poured from his hand and disappeared into the pit of fire.

Owen felt suddenly cold.

He reached out to steady himself, and touched the branch of a tree.

There was no sign of the spaceship anywhere.

Chapter Six
Boxes

Owen raced through the door.

"Grandad!"

"There you are, Owen," said Grandad appearing from the kitchen. "Have you seen what I've got?" said Grandad, smiling.

"I haven't got time, Grandad. Have you seen my teeth?"

"What are you on about, Owen?"

"My teeth, Grandad, I've lost some teeth!"

"But that's what I'm trying to tell you. Have you seen my teeth?"

Owen looked.

Grandad had shiny, new, white teeth.

"That's what I'm trying to say. When I went for my teeth this morning there was a strange pair in the glass. Didn't recognise 'em at all. They really hurt when I put them in."

"But Grandad, where are they, the teeth?"

"Well, here's me new ones, I keep telling you. Those funny ones were no good to me. So I left them at the dentist."

* * *

"I don't get it!" said Chaz, during history.

"Are you completely nuts?" added Freddie.

"I'm telling you what happened," said Owen. "You've got to help me, or he'll come back and . . ."

"And what?"

"Never mind . . . but we've just got to find those teeth."

"Well, I still think you're nuts," said Freddie.

* * *

The day seemed to last for ever. At last the bell went for the end of school. After a

44

short walk Owen, Chaz and Freddie were soon standing outside a white building. Over the door the sign said, *Dentist*.

"You go in."

"No, you, it's your teeth that are missing."

"They're not my teeth, stupid. They're the alien's teeth!"

"So you keep saying!"

"Let's all go."

Owen, followed by Freddie and Chaz, marched into the dentist's reception. A lady in a white coat looked up from a computer screen.

"Have you an appointment?"

"Not exactly, no," said Owen.

"Would you like me to make one for you, then?"

"No, not really."

The woman looked over the top of her glasses.

"You see," Owen carried on, "my grandad's lost some teeth. Well, they're not exactly his teeth . . ."

The woman glared at the boys and pointed to the door. They filed out in a hurry, banging the door behind them.

"What now?" said Freddie.

"Home," said Chaz, "there's a match on the telly."

"We can't just give up," spluttered
Owen. "Come on, I've got an idea."

Ducking down, Owen made his way round
to the back of the building. Freddie and
Chaz followed.

"What are you doing?" hissed Chaz.

"You're going to get us into a lot of
trouble," said Freddie.

Owen took no notice. He bobbed his
head up and looked in the window. There
was a man in a white coat bending over
someone sitting in a large, padded chair.

"What can you see?" whispered Chaz.

"It's just the dentist," said Owen, "let's
try the next window."

In the next room was another dentist, a woman with thick-rimmed glasses. The room after that was smaller, with a sink and mops and a bucket. It had a small window which was open a little.

The room after that was full of boxes. They all had labels: toothpaste, toothbrushes, braces, repairs, fillings. A few metal tools lay on a table along with a jar of white paste. Next to it was a box overflowing with sets of teeth.

"Got it!" said Owen.

"I don't get it!" said Freddie.

"Look, that box is full of false teeth, old ones," said Owen. "Grandad said he took his old teeth to the dentist's surgery. Our teeth are in that box! We just need to get in."

Returning to the smallest window Owen tried to climb in, but he was too big.

"Come on, Freddie, you'll fit."

"Why me?" said Freddie.

"Because you're the right size."

"But what if somebody comes?"

"Go on Fred, we'll keep a look out," said Chaz.

Owen reached in and unlatched the window. Chaz put his back against the wall and gave Freddie a leg up. Freddie slid into the room head first.

There was a clatter as he disappeared from view. Then he appeared at the window wearing a yellow bucket over his head. He

blundered into the wall knocking over some
mops and brooms. They hit the floor with a
clatter.

"Stop mucking about, Fred," laughed Chaz.

"Ssshhh! Not so much noise," hissed Owen.

Freddie took the bucket from his head and glared back at them from the window. Owen made signs to Freddie to go to the next room.

Freddie opened the door and disappeared into the corridor.

Chapter Seven
Tea and Teeth

"Come on, this way," whispered Owen.

Owen and Chaz crouched down and ran back to the last room. They bobbed their heads up and looked in.

"Good," said Owen, "still empty."

Seconds later the door opened and Freddie, looking very worried, walked in and gently closed the door behind him.

Owen gave him the thumbs up and pointed at the box on the table. Freddie seemed to get the idea. He went over and began taking out sets of teeth and holding them up for Owen to see. He had only picked up three or four when he stopped and glared back at the window.

"Don't stop!" mouthed Owen through the glass.

Freddie held up a set of false teeth and held his nose. The teeth were clearly a bit smelly. Secretly, Owen was glad it was Freddie in there, and not him.

"Keep going," called Owen, pointing back at the box.

Chaz waved at Freddie and grinned. He was enjoying the show.

Reluctantly, Freddie carried on. He lifted each set of teeth up, holding them with a finger and thumb, no more. Owen looked closely at each one before shaking his head. Freddie then dropped them on the floor out of the way.

It seemed to take for ever.

Then the box was empty.

Freddie looked at Owen and shrugged.

Owen pressed his face against the glass and ran a hand through his hair. He felt defeated.

Then everything happened at once.

The door to the room opened and a man in a white coat walked in. He was carrying a mug of tea in his hand. When the man saw Freddie he dropped his tea in surprise.

Then Owen saw it.

On the shelf behind Freddie was a large jar.

In the jar was a set of teeth . . . the alien teeth.

Owen banged on the window hard.

The man looked at Owen, startled.

Freddie looked at Owen, terrified.

"Behind you - on the shelf," shouted Owen, pointing frantically.

Freddie looked up and saw the jar. He grabbed it from the shelf and scooted around the table. The man in the white coat saw where Freddie was heading, and stepped across to block the way.

He did not know the floor was covered in teeth as well as the tea he had spilt.

It was like skating on crabs. The man's feet seemed to go in three directions at once. He fell forwards, skidding on his stomach towards Freddie.

Eyes wide with surprise, Freddie jumped in the air. The man in the white

coat slid underneath him like a child on a toboggan. Then, scrambling over the wet teeth, Freddie darted to the door, clutching the jar tightly under one arm.

"Phew! That was close," said Freddie, when they were safely back at the den.

"Is there a funny smell in here?" sniffed Chaz.

"Ha ha, very funny!"

"Freddie, you were fantastic," said Owen. He felt like hugging him, but settled for a friendly pat on the back.

"Now what?" asked Chaz.

"Now we hang on to the teeth until the end of the week. That's when Zarg returns and I'll hand them over."

"Can we come?" said Freddie. "After all, I got them back, didn't I?"

"I thought you didn't believe me, about the alien."

"Well, maybe we didn't. But if we come with you we can find out," said Chaz.

"Why don't we do it now?" asked Freddie.

"I don't think that's a good idea. Zarg said one week. He's not the sort of alien you want to upset."

"How can he be upset if we deliver his teeth early? He might give us a reward, or something."

"But he won't be there . . . he said a week, that's . . . Saturday."

"Well, if he's not there, it won't matter, will it?" said Chaz.

"At least you can show us where you saw the spaceship," said Freddie.

"I really think I should take them home," said Owen, anxiously.

"But that's where you lost them in the first place, remember?" said Chaz, picking up the jar. "Besides, if you hand them over now, you don't have to worry about them anymore, do you? Come on." And with that he skipped out of the den, the jar tucked neatly under his arm.

Chapter Eight
Farmer Stockett

"How long?" asked Emperor Zarg, drumming his fingers on the transparent desk in front of him.

"Just plotting our course back to that planet where you dropped your false teeth," replied the alien at the control desk.

"I didn't drop them. They fell out of my mouth when I was startled by a strange

earth creature," said the Emperor.

"Our holographic data-files say that was a squirrel."

"Yes, well, it was a particularly big and scary one," said Zarg, sulkily.

The alien made no reply. He carried on tapping information into a key pad which hovered in front of his fingers.

"What's taking so long, anyway?" snapped Zarg.

"Er, I think we should have turned left at the Seven Moons of Octar. Still, not to worry, we'll be there in good time to pick up your teeth before heading back."

"You had better not be late, that's all. I have to be at The Inter-Galactic Alien

Council by the eleven orbits of Plutor. I can't be seen there without my teeth."

Princess Altar walked in to the room and stood at her father's side.

"Don't worry, Father, everything will be alright. The Earthchild can be trusted to do as you have commanded."

"Perhaps you are right, my daughter. As for that Earthling, I wouldn't want to be in his shoes, if he has not found my teeth!"

"I'm sure they are safe and sound, all ready and waiting for your return, Father."

"But if he has not . . . " Zarg stood up and bellowed so loudly that the walls of the spaceship shook. "If he has not, then . . ." Zarg threw his head back and a ball of fire shot from his mouth. Some purple plants nearby exploded in a cloud of smoke, leaving a small pile of ash on the floor.

* * *

It was getting dark as the boys set off across the fields towards Stockett's Farm. Owen stared hard at the sky above the tall trees of the woods. He half expected the spaceship to appear. Freddie and Chaz could tell Owen was jumpy.

"I . . . am . . . an . . . alien . . . from . . . outer-space," said Freddie, in his best alien voice. He pulled down the skin under his eyes and stuck his tongue out.

"Pack it in," said Owen. "Here, give me the jar if you're going to mess about."

Just then something swooped low over their heads. Freddie ducked and Chaz dived out of the way. It was Owen's turn to laugh. "It's only an owl."

Chaz climbed out of the ditch he had just fallen into, and Freddie gave a shiver.

All three boys watched the bird disappear silently into the shadows of the wood.

And then something stepped out of the trees. A dark shape, the size of a large man was coming towards them, holding something in its hand.

"What are you boys doing on my land!"

"Farmer Stockett!"

"Quick!"

"Run!"

Freddie and Chaz scrambled back along the track. Owen followed, the teeth-jar banging against his side as he ran. The angry shouts of the farmer could be heard close behind.

"Quick, over the gate," said Freddie.

"Faster, he's catching up!"

Freddie and Chaz both saw the fallen tree branch and jumped it easily, like two hurdlers in a race.

Owen looked back at the wrong moment. He hit the tree branch with his shin and gave a yelp. The jar flew from his hand and bounced along the ground. It hit the fence with the sound of splintering glass.

Something flew into the air and sailed over the hedge.

In the next field a sheep coughed.

Chapter Nine

A Sheep called Dolly

Owen stood still, blinking in the direction the jar had gone.

"Come on Owen. The farmer's coming," shouted Chaz.

"I can't . . . I can't just leave them."

"You won't find them in the dark, will you?"

"He's right, Owen. We'll come back in the morning. Come on!"

"You young rascals, trespassing on my land," yelled Farmer Stockett, waving his stick.

"He wouldn't use that, would he?" said Owen.

"Do you want to wait to find out?"

With the panting figure of Farmer Stockett almost upon them, the boys raced for the gate. Scrambling over, they disappeared onto the patch of waste ground that led to safety, and home.

* * *

It was Saturday. The boys met at the den and walked across the waste ground, over the three fields and back towards Stockett's Farm.

When they arrived, Owen gasped. Everywhere they looked they could see people, cars, lorries and animals. Flags and bunting hung from every tree.

"Oh no," groaned Owen.

"I forgot about this," said Chaz. "It's the Village Show. Come on, it'll be a laugh."

"Don't you see," said Owen, "we'll never find the teeth with all this lot here."

"Well, we can come back tomorrow, can't we?"

"I might not be here tomorrow. If I don't find Zarg's teeth and return them by midday today, I'll be served up on alien toast!"

"Well it's only ten-o-clock. We've got time to try some of the stalls, haven't we?" said Chaz.

"Perhaps we'll think of something while we're going round," said Freddie.

"I suppose so," muttered Owen, gloomily.

There was plenty to see.

All around the edge of the field were stalls and sideshows. There was hoopla, skittles, a coconut-shy and a throw-the-wellie competition.

On the far side of the field several pens had been fenced off.

Groups of men in jackets and caps stood around looking at sheep, pigs, goats and chickens.

Stalls under bright striped canvas sold farm produce: eggs, milk, jam, cheese, fruit and vegetables.

Freddie and Chaz stopped several times to have a go at something. Chaz managed to throw the wellington boot over the hedge; the man in charge did not seem very pleased.

"Don't forget why we're here!" said Owen, rather crossly.

"The teeth, we haven't forgotten," said Chaz.

"No, 'course we haven't . . . hey, look at that helter-skelter!"

Owen sighed. He watched the boys go, and began to wander around the edge of the field hoping to recognise the spot where they were last night. It was dark then, and now the field was full of people, cars and animals. It was like looking for a needle in a haystack.

"Ladies and gentlemen," a crackly voice echoed across the field, "testing, one, two, three . . . is this working?" The voice tried again. "Ladies and gentleman, I'd like to welcome you to our annual village show. I hope you are enjoying yourselves. There's plenty to see and do . . ."

The voice droned on and Owen was hardly listening.

"We hope that our special guest, Garth Vapour, star of Alien Invasion, will be here soon to open the show. And now, if you would like to make your way to the main arena, the best pets competition is about to start."

Owen slowly made his way towards the middle of the field where an orange rope marked out a square patch of grass.

In the middle stood a row of children each clutching their prized pet. There was a girl with a pony tail holding the reins of a small horse, a girl in pig-tails cuddling an extremely long-haired cat, and she stood

next to a boy clutching a tiny mouse. Then
there was a large boy carrying a pig; a little
girl with her arms wrapped around a goldfish
bowl; a tall boy with multi-coloured hair
dangled a parrot in a cage from one hand; a
round faced boy held a bulldog on a lead.
Last of all a girl with frizzy hair had a sheep
on a smart red harness. The sheep wore its
name on its bright red collar: Dolly.

A large lady in a yellow coat was walking along the line followed closely by a man in a brown suit. They both carried clipboards and pencils. Owen thought they must be the judges. He was not very interested in the pet competition and was about to wander on when the crackly voice started up again.

"Well everyone, what a surprise. It looks as if our special guest has arrived early . . . and in costume too!"

Owen looked over to the platform. A man in a straw hat and white jacket was holding a microphone.

Standing next to him was Emperor Zarg.

Chapter Ten
Cat and Mouse

Owen looked around him.

No one was screaming, or running away. Most people were actually smiling.

"It's really nice to have you with us today . . . Mr, er?"

"I'm Zarg, Emperor, Lord High Excellency of the Third Galaxy," said the alien.

A few people giggled.

"And have you a message for everyone here today?" asked the man.

"I have come from the far side of the universe to claim what is mine."

"That sounds pretty important."

"Indeed it is. If I do not have what belongs to me by midday today . . ."

"Then what?"

"I shall destroy your planet."

"Oh, dear," chuckled the man with the microphone.

"Let's give him a big hand, shall we everyone. And thanks for coming along."

Everyone clapped. A few people were laughing. Small children giggled and pointed at the funny man.

Zarg looked a little taken aback. This was not the sort of thing that usually happened when he threatened to destroy planets. These Earthlings were either very brave, or rather stupid.

Owen looked around anxiously. He looked at his watch. It was five minutes-to-twelve. He must find Freddie and Chaz and he must find the teeth.

He left the arena and darted into the crowd, looking in all directions.

All around him people were playing and laughing or munching on burgers and candy-floss. All unaware of the danger only minutes away!

"Freddie!"

Owen spotted Freddie and Chaz. Chaz was about to throw a hoop over a green blow-up alien. Owen grabbed his arm just as he was about to throw.

"Hey, I was about to win that!" spluttered Chaz.

"Never mind that," snapped Owen. "Come this way and I'll show you a real one."

Owen dragged the two boys through the crowd, bumping into several people on the way.

"Hey, watch where you're going."

"Sorry . . . in a bit of a hurry."

Back at the arena the prize for the best pet was about to be given.

"Look, up there. That's the alien."

"And the winner is . . . "

"I thought that was Garth Vapour."

"Will you boys be quiet! The result is about to be announced!" hissed a woman with a camera.

"A minute left . . . I've got to find the alien's teeth!"

In the arena the sheep at the end of the line coughed.

Owen had heard a sheep cough somewhere before. He looked hard at it. Dolly the sheep was smiling. There was something odd about its smile. It was wearing Zarg's teeth!

Then everything happened at once. The mouse, who had been resting in its keeper's hands, decided to make a bid for freedom.

The long haired cat, with hungry eyes, leapt to the ground and grabbed the mouse in its mouth.

Excited by the sudden movement, the bulldog began to bark. The noise frightened the parrot which rattled its cage and screeched loudly; the horse kicked its back legs, knocking over the goldfish bowl; the pig broke free and ran in wild circles squealing noisily.

Owen saw his chance.

"Come on!" he yelled.

He ducked under the rope. Freddie and Chaz followed.

"What are we doing?" hissed Freddie.

"We're getting some teeth out of a sheep!"

Owen ran at Dolly the sheep, who was still smiling strangely. Owen grabbed Dolly about the neck. She shook her head and backed away. Owen hung on tightly.

The sheep coughed loudly, and dropped a set of teeth on the grass. Freddie picked them up.

Owen did not wait another second. He snatched the teeth and ran towards the platform.

Back in the arena, children and parents were running in all directions trying to catch their pets. Someone had rescued the mouse and the cat was being led away in disgrace.

Nearby, the church clock began to strike twelve.

"Here, I think these are yours," said Owen.

"You have done well, Earthchild," said Zarg, and popped the teeth into his mouth. He did not seem to mind that they had just been munched on by a sheep.

"I will not see you again," said the Emperor.

"No offence," said Owen, "but that's fine by me."

Zarg smiled. A perfect smile. He turned away from Owen and walked off the stage, quickly disappearing into the crowd.

Stepping up to the platform was a character in purple cape and red tights. Over his face he wore a rubber alien mask.

"Sorry, I'm late everybody!"

"Who are you?" spluttered the man with the microphone.

"It's Garth Vapour," called out a little boy in the crowd.

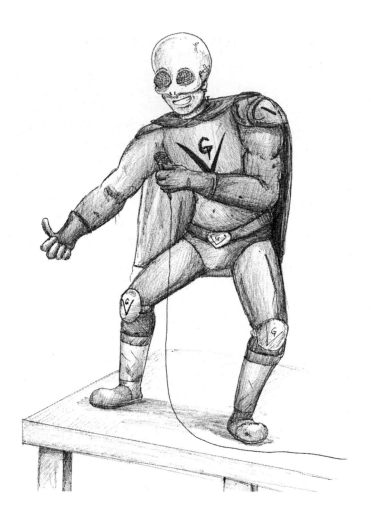

"Sorry, got stuck in traffic," smiled the film star, weakly. "Can't get the spaceship to work like it used to. Now, how about a photo? Anyone?"

Garth Vapour turned to the nearest child on the platform. Clasping Owen by the shoulders, he took a set of plastic alien teeth from his pocket. He held them out to Owen.

"No thanks," said Owen, "I wouldn't trust me with those if I were you."

Also available in the Reluctant Reader Series

Skateboard Gran *(Humorous)*
Ian MacDonald   ISBN 978 1 905637 30 0

Eyeball Soup *(Science Fiction)*
Ian MacDonald   ISBN 978 1 904904 59 5

Chip McGraw *(Cowboy Mystery)*
Ian MacDonald   ISBN 978 1 905637 08 9

Close Call *(Mystery - Interest age 12+)*
Sandra Glover   ISBN 978 1 905 637 07 2

Beastly Things in the Barn *(Humorous)*
Sandra Glover   ISBN 978 1 904904 96 0
www.sandraglover.co.uk

Cracking Up *(Humorous)*
Sandra Glover   ISBN 978 1 904904 86 1

Deadline *(Adventure)*
Sandra Glover   ISBN 978 1 904904 30 4

The Crash *(Mystery)*
Sandra Glover   ISBN 978 1 905637 29 4

The Owlers *(Adventure)*
Stephanie Baudet   ISBN 978 1 904904 87 8

The Curse of the Full Moon *(Mystery)*
Stephanie Baudet   ISBN 978 1 904904 11 3

A Marrow Escape *(Adventure)*
Stephanie Baudet   ISBN 1 900818 82 5

The One That Got Away *(Humorous)*
Stephanie Baudet   ISBN 1 900818 87 6

The Haunted Windmill *(Mystery)*
Margaret Nash   ISBN 978 1 904904 22 9

Trevor's Trousers *(Humorous)*
David Webb   ISBN 978 1 904904 19

The Library Ghost *(Mystery)*
David Webb   ISBN 978 1 904374 66

Dinosaur Day   *(Adventure)*
David Webb   ISBN 978 1 904374 67 1

There's No Such Thing As An Alien *(Science Fiction)*
David Webb   ISBN 1 900818 66 3

Laura's Game   *(Football)*
David Webb   ISBN 1 900818 61 2

Grandma's Teeth   *(Humorous)*
David Webb   ISBN 978 1 905637 20 1

Snakes Legs and Cows Eggs *(Humorous)*
Adam Bushnell   ISBN 978 1 905637 21 8

PRINT

PUBLISHING

www.eprint.co.uk